Cats Are Merely Dragons that Simply Choose to Hide

BY D. R. St. John IV

RoseDog ❧ Books

PITTSBURGH, PENNSYLVANIA 15222

RoseDog Books
701 Smithfield Street
Pittsburgh, PA 15222
Visit our website at www.rosedogbookstore.com

ISBN: 978-1-4809-0224-4
eISBN: 978-1-4809-0517-7

I owe the dream of mine to three wonderful women.
The first is my Muse who pushed me to enter the writing contest
and win first place. Shelly, thank you.
The second was Sharlene Wallace who was my cheeleader.
She never gave up cheering me on.
The third and most important was my wife, Vicki L. St. John.
She was my supporter, my rock and the love of my life. Thank you sweetheart.

Foreword

On a warm summer night under my open skylight, I was reading a book and stroking my purring cat. Suddenly, my cat spotted a tiny bat that had flown in to pay us a visit. We had several cats at that time so I was privileged to witness a room full of leaping cats vainly attempting to catch our uninvited guest. I sat down on the floor to watch the spectacle from a cats-eye view. I was awed by their acrobatic performance. Then I noticed that one of the smaller cats was busy chasing something that I couldn't see. Another was sitting on the armchair growling at something only visible to him. At that moment I realized that this wasn't normal behavior for any other animal. What kind of animal would act like these cats? My mother once told me that things are not always what they seem. She also told me about the noble Dragons of long, long ago. That's when the secret hit me. **Cats are merely Dragons that simply Choose to Hide.**

Their golden scales

have given way,

to the furry tails

we see today.

Fierce battles

with noble knights,

now skirmishes

with birds and mice.

Yet look you now
in eyes of green
and ancient times
might still be seen.

Because,

Cats are merely Dragons,

that simply choose to hide!

On moonlit nights,

those phantom flights,

with things that

can't be seen.

They're really things

with fairy wings;

old friends of ancient times.

See, Dragon friends
are Magical beings,
that travel between
those times.

I tell you,

Cats are merely Dragons,

that simply choose to hide!

Hissing lizards

and kitty wizards,

their sounds are much alike.

A Tiger's roar

is a Dragon's score,

whose melody is fright.

Listen, I know,

Cats are merely Dragons,

that simply choose to hide!

Haven't you seen a cat
that flings its body
through the air?

It's almost as though,

once long ago,

Magical wings

carried them here and there.

Trust me and you'll see it,
Cats are merely Dragons
that simply choose to hide!

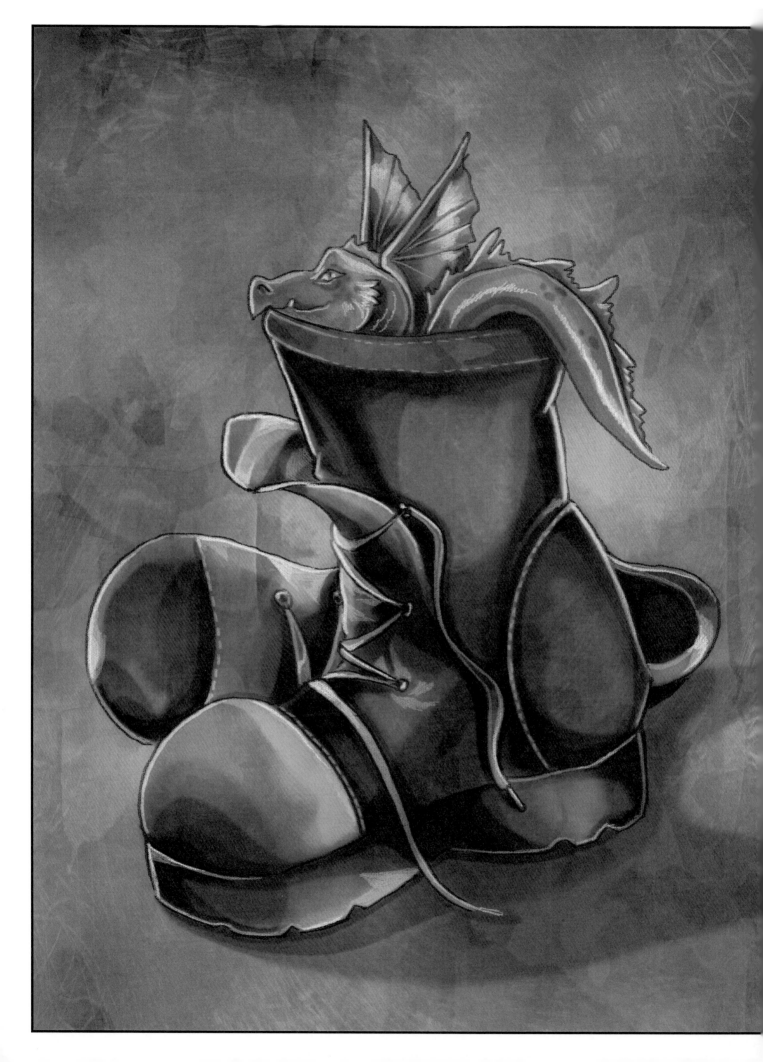

Now think you not,

a dread solemn thought,

that Dragons have,

now ceased.

For deep inside,

your feline's hide

there dwells

that Noble Beast,

As you now know,

Cats are merely Dragons

that simply choose to hide...

...for now!